SUSAN GATES

Fisherwitch

Illustrated by Rhian Nest James

For Phillip Rashidi

Scholastic Children's Books,
Commonwealth House, 1-19 New Oxford Street,
London WC1A 1NU, UK
a division of Scholastic Ltd
London ~ New York ~ Toronto ~ Sydney ~ Auckland

Published in the UK by Scholastic Ltd, 1998

Text copyright © Susan Gates, 1998
Illustrations © Rhian Nest James, 1998

ISBN 0 590 19106 3

Typeset by Backup Creative Services, Dorset
Printed by Cox & Wyman Ltd, Reading, Berks

2 4 6 8 10 9 7 5 3 1

Fisherwitch

"Come back, Moses," I yell at my brother. "There's something funny going on here. Something I don't like at all."

Moses stops. For once, I think to myself, he's going to do as he's told.

But then, from out of the reeds, comes the strangest thing of all. It looks like a ball. But it's floating above the ground like a bright blue cloud. It glows like a jewel. And a thousand tiny rainbows are sparkling in it.

More fantastic Young Hippo Magic stories!

My Friend's a Gris Quok
Malorie Blackman

Diggory and the Boa Conductor
The Little Pet Dragon
Philippa Gregory

Broomstick Removals
Broomstick Services
Ann Jungman

The Cleaning Witch
Cecilia Lenagh

Hello Nellie and the Dragon
Elizabeth Lindsay

The Marmalade Pony
Linda Newbery

Mr Wellington Boots
Ann Ruffell

The Wishing Horse
Malcolm Yorke

Three more great stories by Susan Gates:

Esther and the Baby Baboon
Pet Swapping Day
Whizz Bang and the Crocodile Room

Chapter 1

It's the hot season in our part of
Africa. The lake near our village is
drying up. Sensible people stay indoors
or go out under umbrellas to keep off
the sun.

But my little brother Moses isn't
sensible. He keeps pestering me. "Come
out and play with me, Precious."

5

My mum is at the market. My dad is mending his fishing nets. So I've got to look after Moses.

"It's too hot to play," I tell him.

But Moses is already running outside into the sunshine.

Grandma's working at her sewing-machine. She looks up and says, "Be careful. It's very hot today. The kind of day when Fisherwitch comes out the lake. Fisherwitches are very sneaky people so keep your eyes open. Keep your ears open. And if you hear anything strange, see anything strange, don't hang around. Run straight back home to me!"

Moses and I laugh. We think it's just one of her stories. Gran has lots of stories about witches and spirits and zombies. If you believed all of them you'd be too scared to go out the door! And, besides, even if the story were true, how could Gran protect us against a witch? She's a tiny, skinny old gran. A puff of wind would blow her away.

"Okay, Gran, okay," we laugh.
"We'll be careful!"

As soon as I step out the house I
smell a revolting pong – a dreadful,
fishy stink.

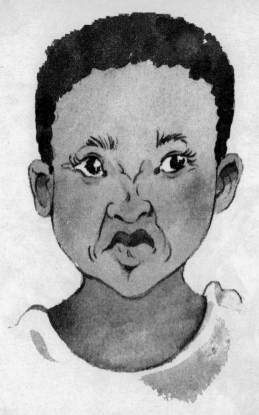

"Phew," says Moses, wrinkling up his nose. "What's that smell?"

I shrug. "I don't know. It's very strange. I've never smelled it before."

Then we hear a strange noise. It's coming from the reeds at the edge of our lake, near the weaver-bird tree.

But weaver-birds don't make noises like that.

Clack, clack, it goes. *Clack, clack.*

Moses is a very inquisitive boy. He wants to know everything that's going on.

"What's that noise?" he says. And he starts walking towards the reeds.

I'm beginning to get worried now.
I'm his big sister and I'm responsible
for him. And I can't help remembering
Gran's warning: "If you hear anything
strange, see anything strange…"

I've just seen something strange!
Right down by my feet. I see ten long

scratches in the sand. I don't know an animal that leaves a trail like that. A hyena doesn't, a crocodile doesn't. And it leads right down to the reeds where the clacking noise is coming from.

"Come back, Moses," I yell at my brother. "There's something funny going on here. Something I don't like at all."

Moses stops. For once, I think to myself, he's going to do as he's told.

But then, from out of the reeds, comes the strangest thing of all. It looks like a ball. But it's floating above the ground like a bright blue cloud. It glows like a jewel. And a thousand tiny rainbows are sparkling in it.

Chapter 2

As soon as Moses sees it he holds out his arms. "What a pretty thing!" he cries. "I want that pretty thing for myself!"

And he runs to catch it.

I feel a chill in my heart. I know that there's danger here somewhere.

"Don't go, Moses." I try to pull

him back.

But Moses is very stubborn. When he wants something he never gives up. He rushes after the beautiful blue ball.

It floats away, just out of his reach.

Moses runs to grab it. He's almost touching it! But it darts away in a blue flash, quick as a kingfisher. It won't let him catch it. Every time he gets close it whisks away. He chases it.

And it's leading him closer and closer to the reeds by the lake.

"Moses," I shout. "Come back. This is some kind of trick. I'm sure it is!"

But Moses takes no notice. The
shiny blue ball disappears into the
reeds. And Moses runs after it.

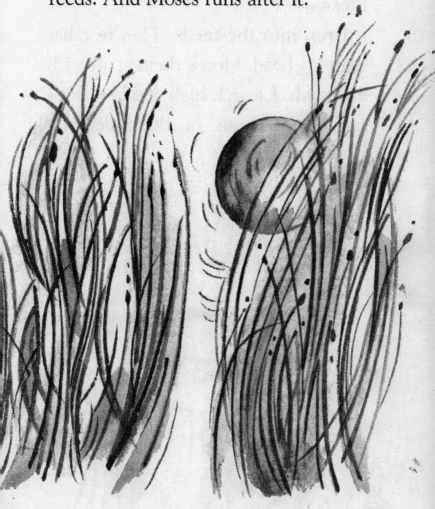

There is silence for two seconds. Then Moses yells, "Precious, help me, Precious!"

I run into the reeds. They're taller than my head. I force them apart with my hands. I search high and low. But I can't find Moses or the blue ball.

They've both vanished. And all that's left is a fishy pong and ten snaky tracks…

I can't think what to do. I yell, "Moses, Moses!"

No answer.

I rush back home. But my mum isn't back, or my dad. Only Grandma's here and she's too old to help.

"Moses followed a blue ball!" I tell her. "He went after it into the reeds and I can't find him!"

Grandma looks up quickly from her sewing. She narrows her eyes.

"Did this ball dance in the air?" she asks. "And did it dart away when Moses got close?"

"Yes, yes."

"Then Fisherwitch is back!" says Gran. "She's back hunting for children. I told you to be careful! That ball Moses followed was a witchball. Fisherwitch uses them to catch children. When children chase them, they run right into her trap!"

"I smelled a fishy smell!" I tell Gran. "I heard something go *Clack, clack*. I saw ten snaky tracks!"

"That's Fisherwitch all right," says Gran. "Those are the tracks of her long sharp nails. Her nails that go *Clack, clack*. Quick, we must hurry. There's no time to lose. If we don't hurry, we'll never see Moses again!"

We rush outside. My heart's beating very fast. "Please let us be in time," I whisper to myself.

Grandma sniffs. She sniffs again. "I know that smell," she says. "That pong of rotting fish. I haven't smelled it for fifty years. But it's a smell you never forget. Fisherwitch is definitely back!"

Chapter 3

We creep along the lake shore.

"Shhhh!" says Grandma.

She parts some tall reeds.

I peep through. And see a fearful sight.

It's Fisherwitch. She's fast asleep. She's naked as a hippo, old and lumpy as a baobab tree. She's big as an elephant. Her skin is grey and baggy like an elephant's skin. Little red crabs are running in and out of its folds.

Phew, the pong is awful! You would need a whole shopful of perfume to make her sweet again!

She's got long yellow nails, as long as the canoes that fish on our lake. Her nails drag on the ground. They're very sharp, like spears.

She's made herself a shelter of fish-bones to shade her from the sun.

"Where are you, Moses?" whispers Gran. "Are you round here somewhere?"

Fisherwitch snores. Tiny shrimps tumble out her hair.

My heart's beating so loud I'm scared it will wake her.

Can YOU read four Young Hippo books?

YOUNG HIPPO Readometer

The Young Hippo is sending a special prize to everyone who collects any four of these stickers, which can be found in Young Hippo books.

This is one sticker to stick on your own Young Hippo Readometer Card!

Collect four stickers and fill up your Readometer Card

There are all these stickers to collect too!

Get your Young Hippo Readometer Card from your local bookshop, or by sending your name and address to:

Young Hippo Readometer Card Requests, Scholastic Children's Books, 6th Floor, Commonwealth House, 1-19 New Oxford Street, London WC1A 1NU

Offer begins March 1997

This offer is subject to availability and is valid in the UK and the Republic of Ireland only.

Then we hear a very small voice. "Here I am. I'm trapped in her nails."

Fisherwitch has put her long nails together, like a cage. A big, frightened eye peeps out from inside. It's my brother Moses!

"I can't get out!" he says.

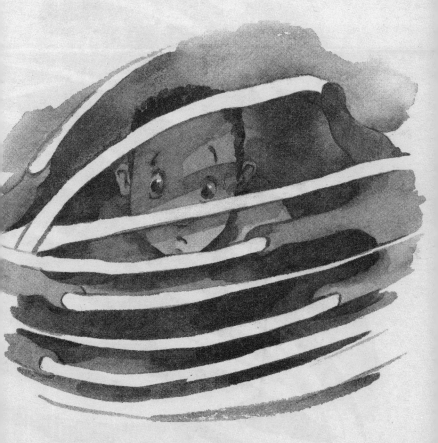

He pokes his fingers through the bars of his cage. I creep forward. I can hold his hand, but I can't get him out.

"What do we do now?" I beg Gran. I'm almost crying.

But Gran doesn't cry. She stays cool.

There's a fierce look in her eyes. A look I haven't seen before.

"Come with me," she hisses. She pulls me away.

"We can't leave Moses."

"We're coming straight back. But we must hurry. If Fisherwitch wakes up..."

I have to let go of Moses' fingers. "Don't leave me!" he says. But I have to run after Gran.

"What will she do with him?" I ask Gran. "What will she do with my brother?"

Gran's voice is grim. "She plans to eat him," she says.

"Oh, no!"

"Oh, yes. She will definitely eat him, unless we can save him. A Fisherwitch doesn't often catch children. Usually they catch fish. They stab them with their long, sharp nails. They thread fish on their nails like shish kebabs.

Sometimes they have twenty silver fish flapping on each of their nails! And they munch them, bones and all, when they feel like a snack. But when it gets very hot and the lake starts to dry up and there aren't many fish, then Fisherwitch gets hungry. Her belly begins to rumble. And she comes into the villages, hunting for children!"

"She won't shish kebab Moses, will she?"

"She will," says Gran, "unless we stop her. And if she doesn't shish kebab him straight away, she'll drag him into the lake. Like crocodiles do. She'll take him down to her dark cave. And keep him prisoner there until she feels like nibbling something."

"How do you know all this about Fisherwitches?" I ask Gran as we hurry back to our house.

"That's another story," says Gran. "No time for it now. Fisherwitch will soon wake up. Her belly will rumble. And then – no more Moses!"

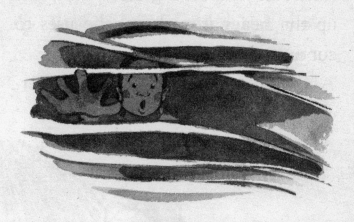

Chapter 4

I stumble after Gran. In my mind I can see my brother's poor frightened eyes, his tiny fingers reaching through the fingernail cage. But what can we do? We're helpless against the power of Fisherwitch.

But my little gran isn't helpless. She's fierce and determined. She rushes to her sewing-machine, picks up the heavy iron shears she uses to cut material.

"Quick, quick!" she says. "Fisher-witch is waking up!"

"How do you know?"

"Listen!"

I hear it too. A noise like a lion's roar: *GRRRRRRR!* It makes the ground shake. It's coming out of the reeds. It's Fisherwitch's empty belly, rumbling.

We run back. We trample through the reeds. Fisherwitch isn't awake yet. But she's twitching in her sleep. She spits out a fish-head.

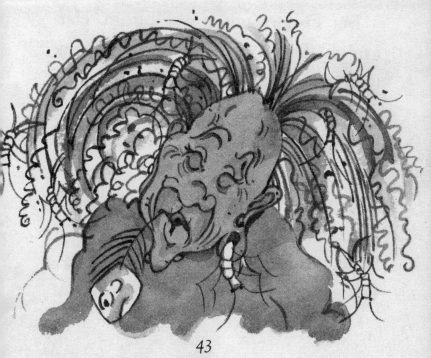

There's no time to lose.

Gran raises her shears high. They glitter in the sun. She begins to hack through Fisherwitch's nails. It's very hard work – they're tough as elephants' toenails.

I hold my breath. One nail falls off! Moses pokes out his arm. "I'm nearly free!"

But Fisherwitch is waking up. Her eyelids flutter. One slides up. I see a cold, green eye swivel in our direction.

Grandma doesn't panic. She carries on cutting. Snap, snap. Another nail falls to the sand.

"I'm free!" says Moses. He wriggles out of his cage.

Fisherwitch yawns. With one long, yellow nail she scratches her itchy

places. Then she tries to scratch her back. But there's no nail to scratch with! My gran has just cut it off.

Fisherwitch is suddenly wide awake. She screams with rage. She stands up, in a shower of fish scales all green and gold.

"Who has cut my nails?" she howls.
"My beautiful long nails. And who has
stolen my dinner?"

Then she spots us, just as we're
creeping off through the reeds.

"You!" she hisses. "You cut my
nails!"

She's hopping mad! Blue fire sizzles
from her eyes.

"Run, run," says Gran.

But Fisherwitch is right behind!

She's howling, spitting fish-bones.
She's got eight nails left and they're all
sharp as spears.

We run towards our village, dragging Moses with us. But however fast we run, Fisherwitch is on our heels. *Thud, thud, thud!* For a big old witch she can run very fast!

"Help, help, save us!" But no one hears. They're all indoors, where it's nice and cool.

Fisherwitch is jabbing at us – trying to stab us like fish. Soon we'll be flapping on those long sharp nails!

But our house is right here. We tumble inside. Push a bed against the door, then sit down on it, gasping for breath.

Chapter 5

"We're safe now," I say. "She can't get us now!"

"I wouldn't be too sure," says Gran.

There's a scratching noise going up the walls.

"What's that?" says Moses, his eyes wide with fear.

Clack, clack, clack, clack, go

Fisherwitch's nails.

"She's climbing on to the roof," says
Grandma.

Sharp yellow claws come sliding
through our grass roof. They jab about
trying to find us.

They stab a water-melon and a sack
of maize.

"Ah ha, got you!" screams Fisher-witch.

Moses and I dive under the bed.

But Gran isn't scared. "I'll tell you, shall I," she says, "how I know so much about Fisherwitches?"

"Now is no time for stories!" I shout from under the bed.

Jab, jab, go Fisherwitch's nails. She stabs the mattress and hauls it up through the roof.

"Get under the bed, Gran!" I beg.

But Gran will not hide. She stands strong as a termites' nest. And shouts out her story so Fisherwitch, squatting up on our roof, can hear her.

"Do you remember, Fisherwitch?" calls Gran. "Fifty years ago when you last came to this village? And you stole

a little girl called Rosebud? She had braids and blue beads in her hair? Well, that little girl was my best friend. And I've been waiting all this time, Fisherwitch, for you to pay another visit."

My tiny gran takes out her heavy iron shears. With eight swift blows she chops off every one of Fisherwitch's nails.

"Aieee!" screams Fisherwitch from the roof. "You have killed me!"

Then there is silence. We wait a long time. Very cautiously, we open the door and peep out of the house.

There's nothing outside but a blue witchball. It's floating high above the ground.

"Don't you chase it this time," I warn Moses.

"I'm not that stupid!" he says.

The witchball hovers above us for a moment. It darts away, high into the sky. It goes higher, higher until it's just a blue dot. Then, with a bright orange flash, it burns up in the sun.

"Is she dead?" I ask Gran.

"Who knows?" says Gran. "Fisher-witches are very sneaky people. She might be dead. And she might not. She might hide out somewhere until her nails grow again."

I shiver. "I hope she's *really* dead."

"Well, if she isn't and she comes hunting children we know what to do."

My fierce little gran lifts up her iron shears. They glitter in the sun. *Snap, snap,* they go. *Snap, snap!*

The End